The Number Chronicles

Edited By Byron Tobolik

First published in Great Britain in 2023 by:

Young Writers
Remus House
Coltsfoot Drive
Peterborough
PE2 9BF
Telephone: 01733 890066
Website: www.youngwriters.co.uk

Book Design by Ashley Janson

Softback ISBN 978-1-80459-919-8

Printed and bound in the UK by BookPrintingUK
Website: www.bookprintinguk.com
YB0564M

FOREWORD

For our latest competition, Integer, we asked secondary school students to take inspiration from numbers in the world around them and create a story. Whether it's racing against a deadline, cracking a mysterious code, or writing about the significance of a certain date, the authors in this anthology have taken this idea and run with it, writing stories to entertain and inspire. Even the format they were challenged to write within - a mini saga, a story told in just 100 words - shows that numeric influence is all around! With infinite numbers, there are infinite possibilities...

The result is a thrilling and absorbing collection of tales written in a variety of styles, and it's a testament to the creativity of these young authors.

Here at Young Writers it's our aim to inspire the next generation and instill in them a love of creative writing, and what better way than to see their work in print? The imagination and skill within these pages show just a fraction of the writing skill of the next generation, and it's proof that we might just be achieving that aim! Congratulations to each of these fantastic authors, they should be very proud of themselves.

CONTENTS

Consett Academy, Consett

Longdean School, Bennetts End

Madni Academy, Savile Town

Ysgol Bryn Alyn, Gwersyllt

THE STORIES

THERE WAS
1 MILE
TO GO...

IT WAS FRIDAY
13TH...

I'D WON
£1 MILLION...

I GOT MY
15
MINUTES OF
FAME...

I WAS
NUMBER
9...

IT WAS THE
LESSER OF
2 EVILS...

IT WAS IN
LOCKER
876...

1 OF US WAS
LYING...

Unlocked

Ring, ring, ring.
"Hello, Detective Killings here."
5 minutes later, we were on our way. I arrived, ready for my new case: unlocking a phone for a murder investigation. Her birthday was Friday 13th May - *13.05.1999*. I tried that. *Error.* I took it to the office and tried to crack the code. I arrived back at the office and connected the phone to my computer and waited for the password to be cracked. There were 8 numbers. The first 3 were *492*. I needed 5 more. It took ages.
2 hours later, 1 number left. It was *49258219*. Unlocked.

Grace Robson (12)
Burford School, Burford

To The Moon!

The 2 astronauts were ready to launch. The astronauts' eyes were filled with horror as they looked out of the bulletproof windows wondering if they would ever see their children's faces again. They were off the Earth, still missing their families and wondering if they would ever be able to go back to Earth. The 2 astronauts could feel the power of the rocket going through their veins. Suddenly, the cabin was losing oxygen every second. The astronauts looked at their watches on their wrists. Then they stopped breathing and they realised they wouldn't see their families ever again.

Dawson Steele (12)
Burford School, Burford

The Telephone

The telephone began to chime again. The number showed one word: *Eight.* With trembling hands and blurry sight, I reached for the phone and picked it up. A cold, stern voice bellowed down the line, "Where's my ransom? Where's my money?" But all I could do was stand in petrified silence as the man continued, "You promised! You know the consequences."
After a long moment of silence, a bang came from the other end. Then, he hung up. I sank into the armchair, knowing what he'd done. He said he'd make me suffer and now I was. She was dead.

Megan Gilbey (12)
Burford School, Burford

13 Is Death

I looked in the mirror, 13 was written large and bold on my forehead. I glanced at the calendar, March 13th was circled, and the previous dates were crossed out. My hands shook nervously as beads of sweat ran down my forehead and dropped onto the floor with a loud drip. There was a shout. "Number 13!" Suddenly, the always locked door opened revealing certain death. The beads of sweat fell onto the floor with a harsh hiss. I wondered what was beneath the ground. Something deadly and evil, for sure. I remembered the screams I heard before. "Step forward..."

Amber Keeling (14)
Burford School, Burford

420

The numbers on the wall changed to 420. I knew my mistake. I had to run. He chased after me. I ran through the woods. *Snap!* The twigs behind me snapped under immense pressure. "Come back 420, I need you! I need your services!" he exclaimed.

"How much?"

No words came. I kept going. My mate, Tom 419, died 2 days ago. I was next. It went dark.

I woke up in a troubled state, inside a prison cell. 420...

A dark voice said, "Tell me what you know about Edward Backland." I fell silent.

"No," I muttered.

Albert Pitt (13)
Burford School, Burford

1:30

1:30. I'll always remember that time. The day it all happened. It was a normal school day until it wasn't. Silence filled the classroom. 1, 2, 3... *Bang!* A raging, booming sound pierced my ears. All of a sudden, my worst nightmare came to life. The still room turned into turbulence; screams of pain rang in my ears and drums banged in my head. As I sprinted to the corner, I heard the sound of footsteps getting closer and closer. My heart trembled. Then it happened. As I crouched behind my classmates, my stomach twisted and turned. He was there...

Emily French (13)

Burford School, Burford

The Time Machine

I opened my eyes and looked around. All I could see was number 4. "Step forward, it's your turn next." *Who was that?* I suddenly saw a metal box appear in front of me. It was a time machine! "Step inside." There was that voice again! The door opened. I hesitantly stepped inside. The door slammed behind me. There was a clock on the side of the wall of the time machine. It suddenly went back an hour. The time machine suddenly started to move violently and then halted to a stop. "That's it, my life is over!"

Olivia Hill (12)
Burford School, Burford

My Burger Rage

As I walked in, I saw something terrifying. There were zero Whoppers, zero Cokes and zero chips. I was speechless. I wasn't sure what to do. At that moment, a ringing in my head began. I started to hear a whisper: "No Whoppers, no chips and no Coke makes me *crazy.*" I burst into a rage, smashing bottles, tipping over shelves - I almost killed a Burger King worker. Nothing could stop me. I was drenched in sweat, covered in blood and bruises - but nothing would stop me. Nothing but a Burger King worker ramming a Whopper down my throat.

Michael Broad (13)
Burford School, Burford

Roll The Dice

1... We died. 2, 3, 4, 5... We continued. 6... We survived. All locked up. Gulping back fear. The dice bounced, making clanging sounds on the table. There were 6; 5 competing to survive, 1 controlling the game. Shaky hands reached for the dice. It gently rolled across the table... 1. Silence. Cold shivers rushed down our spines. Now, there were 4. Rolling the dice again and again, we died off like flies. Another 1 was rolled. Only 2 left. We stared at each other. Fear was now an understatement. The dice rolled... *Bang!* It bounced and I was free.

Imogen Thomas (13)
Burford School, Burford

Why Not To Go To School

We were learning about Pythagoras' theorem. My brain was trying to take it all in but all I could think about was my gymnastics competition. Little did I know that I might not compete.
The next day, we were recapping the previous maths lesson when I put my hand up and said something idiotic, "A triangle has 4 sides and the theorem is only for triangles with sides of 13cm."
The whole class laughed at me and my cheeks blushed. Little did I know that those words would unleash the monster and the world would never be the same again.

Isabel Garrett (12)
Burford School, Burford

The Real Princess

It was Friday the 13th and I woke up in my princess bed. Then a butler came in and asked, "Number 20, are you up? Good, you are."

"What do you mean?" I said.

"You are meeting the prince."

"Okay," I replied.

So I got dressed in my amazing gown and had 24 hours to impress the prince. Later that day, when I only had 2 hours left with him, another girl came in and claimed to be me.

"One of you must be lying."

But he knew that I was the girl that would marry him, not that girl.

Hope Duncan (12)
Burford School, Burford

Carrie

"Carrie?" I muttered as a single tear rolled down my cheek. The floorboards creaked as a piercing scream shook the home. I will never get that out of my head. All around me, the glass cabinets clattered, along with the rest of the home. I fell to the floor as a dark figure lurked in the doorway as lightning struck. Rain dripped onto my face as I scrambled to get up onto my feet. Suddenly, the figure began brandishing a knife. I gasped as it took heavy footsteps towards me. I slipped over in the water.
"Carrie... Is that you?"

Charlotte Baldwin (13)
Burford School, Burford

Thirteen Minutes Left

Only 13 minutes left to live. Just 13. No more, no less. The clock ticked menacingly, counting down my life like a time bomb, only stopping at the end. I wish I could change my fate, but it was already decided; set in stone. The eerie silence echoed around as everyone sat slumped against the wall, lost and defeated. If this was a story, this would be the part where we made an epic escape. But this wasn't a story, it was real life and nobody could escape time, not even me. The end had arrived. "Goodbye," I whispered, "goodbye."

Anabelle King (12)
Burford School, Burford

60 In 1

This was the 60th time a villain had attacked this week.

"Ugh, when will this end?" said Peter.

A roar came from the Empire State Building. It was King Kroc. His rough, gnarly skin grated against the spire.

"Ahh, Bug Boy, short time no see!" growled King Kroc.

The neon spider leapt off a short spire. The neon spider uppercut the overgrown reptile. King Kroc threw his claws at him. Peter dodged his every move.

"Missed me, missed me, now you gonna kiss- Actually, never mind," smiled Peter.

Edward Traynor (12)
Burford School, Burford

The Man Next Door

Ding! The clock struck 12. Mr and Mrs Smith and their 2 children were having trouble sleeping. The hotel floors were creaking and the room next door was making strange, loud noises. It went on for a little while and stopped after about 3 hours. Mrs Smith was concerned and even more so because she was a nurse. As she opened the brown door, she heard someone struggling to breathe. When she walked in, she saw a young man pinned against the wall with a gunshot wound. She applied pressure to the wound but unfortunately, she was too late.

Lily Giles (12)
Burford School, Burford

5 Seconds Left!

It was a dark, gloomy da- *Crash!* There goes another one. Why did my country put us in this situation? 5 people from my street had been killed in the last couple of days. World War 5. Surely, they had lost their minds! Half of the population was killed in the last one, me nearly being one of them. *Wait! No! What's that sound?* Looking up, I could see a Sukhoi Su-27 dropping bombs in me and my family's direction. What were we going to do? This was the end. My heart was pounding. 5 seconds left. Goodb- *Boom!*

Samuel Lawrence (11)

Burford School, Burford

The Death Games

Hello, I am number 9 and my friends are 8, 6 and 12. But there are 100 of us. Well, there were loads of us, but most have died because of one of the most dangerous games which we are playing today. Oh no, the buzzer's gone. It's time to play. The few that are left head down to the playing field. The game starts and everyone runs until the word, "Stop!" Someone trips and is shot. They perish. Everyone is now terrified, including me. Everyone starts running. "Stop!" Oh, I feel it coming. I'm going to fall...

Ruby Agg (12)
Burford School, Burford

The Ambush

It was Friday the 13th, 2086. We had started our invasion, taking over the first country on our list. 1. Next, we planned to take Brazil. After multiple weeks of planning, we were ready. After breaking the border, we went straight to the capital, taking out everything in our way. Once we reached Brasilia, it was dead quiet. All we could hear were the trees moving in the wind. Suddenly, there was a huge explosion taking out half of our men. It was an ambush. Guns were being fired from every direction. I ran away, hoping I'd survive.

Jack Williams (12)
Burford School, Burford

60 Seconds To Escape

60, 59, 58, 57... That was how many seconds Max had left to escape. It was dark and spacious. He didn't know where he was. Max was running around the edge of the room looking for a way out. *I'm going to die,* Max thought. This was dangerous. He felt something, something that felt different to the rest of the room. It had big, knobbly parts on the side of it. Max tried pushing, kicking, and pulling. Looking for a keyhole, Max was getting scared. *How long's left?* he thought. 3, 2, 1... It was the end for Max.

Oscar Solomon (12)
Burford School, Burford

We Ended With 1

We started the evening off with 9, we ended with 1. Me. It was supposed to be a fun night in the woods. It wasn't supposed to end like this. Something was off as soon as we stepped foot in the woods. I told my friends that we should leave. "You're being paranoid," they told me and just brushed me off. I would have been more insistent if I knew the night would end with the morning sun rising and my friends' bloody and disembowelled corpses scattered across the ground. We started with 9, ended with 1. Just me left.

Ellie Duncan (13)
Burford School, Burford

Number 9

Bombs dropped from above. I looked around, trying to find somewhere to stay safe. All I could see on the bombs was the number 9. I could hear them ticking but the number on the bomb wasn't moving. I wasn't sure if it was a trap. Suddenly, everything went silent. I knew that wasn't good. *Kapow!* The bombs blew up. Fire everywhere. Instantly, I felt blood gushing from my head. Within 9 seconds, I dropped. Later that week, I woke up on the 9th of December. Doctors said I had to remain in the hospital for months.

Charlie Ward (12)
Burford School, Burford

The Runaway Experiment

I used to be Experiment 44, and that's all I knew. I ran away a year ago and found an ice hockey club. Pretty soon after, I left the lab. The captain, Sasha, saved me when the scientists came for me. They were after me because I was the only successful AI they'd built. They appeared at my 4th game and I found out the other team were the failed experiments. We won but I didn't feel any emotion. Since then, I have been attending school with Sasha and Molly, the assistant captain. I'm Amber Astro and that's my story.

Alexandria Perry (13)
Burford School, Burford

The Endless Tally

I rolled over when I heard the 7am alarm for all the criminals' breakfasts. I was starving until I opened my eyes and saw my cellmate carving a new line on the wall. I focused and saw that the whole room was a massive tally chart. I arrived late last night, she must have been sleeping. I counted 5, 10, 15, 20, 25... The scraped lines were uneven and messy, but still, I couldn't help but stare.
I asked, "How long have you been here?"
She looked at me and said each line resembled a year. Then she laughed.

Kasey Leroux (12)
Burford School, Burford

The Decoy

Have you ever diffused a bomb while falling out of the sky over one of the most famous cities in the world? Well, I have. It all started with my arch-rival Armanie Spighiv, the owner of a sketchy business that dealt in illegal narcotics. I work for a secret intelligence agency, and for the longest time, I've been trying to capture him. So when a ping came up on my radar with the location of Armanie's helicopter, I was straight on it. It was only after 2 minutes, I was informed that it was a decoy helicopter with bombs.

Tristan Kvist (13)
Burford School, Burford

The Jump

"Agent 42; it's now or never," the voice hissed down the line. It was time. My blood was pumping. I knew what I needed to do. I looked behind me. 10 people surrounded me. My stomach was in knots as I looked down at the river 200ft below. *3, 2, 1...*
All I felt was the air swishing through my silky hair. It felt like I'd been falling for ages. I braced my body for impact; holding my breath, tensing my body. I knew that in a matter of seconds, my body would be submerged in an icy-cold bath.

Sam Middleton (12)
Burford School, Burford

The Note

I looked down at the decayed piece of paper, the top of it gave it all away - 13th November 1988. Before I could even read the note, instant shivers shuddered down my spine. The room was so silent that I could hear my own heart rate and my horrified breaths mixed with the odd sounds of water dripping. My eyes glossed over the paper, riddled with droplets of sweat. By this point, I couldn't tell if the dripping was from the neglected room or me. As I read through it thoroughly, I saw it. The words that changed my life...

Foxx Hughes (14)

Burford School, Burford

The Chase

I was already going 100 miles an hour, but so were they. I was in my 3-year-old Ford Fiesta when I heard it... Gunshots! I began to increase my speed and now I was in a bad situation. I was going at maximum speed but that thing wasn't. It was approaching at rapid speed in a mysterious vehicle. At that moment, I realised I was headed straight towards the edge of the Grand Canyon. I slammed on the brakes and the other things went over.
The next second, they began flying and blew up my car. I'm now in hospital.

Charlie Clack (13)
Burford School, Burford

The Bombs

It was busy outside; police cars, fire engines and ambulances. There was a news reporter as well. *It must be serious.* I quickly turned on the news. There was a bomb in the basement. It was unsafe because there were still 11 more bombs in the basement. I went to go and look when I heard a bang. *Were my neighbours now dead?* One of my lifelong friends was gone for good. I had tears in my eyes. My other neighbours were on the news telling a story about how they heard it and called the police. What happened?

Sophie Littlewood-Rix (12)
Burford School, Burford

It Struck 12:00

The clock struck 12:00 and horror struck my eyes. I gathered a pillow and a blanket and hid in a small room behind the wardrobe. It had been some time. However, the clock still said 12:00. Suddenly, the room went dark. There was a cold breeze in the air. Pounding on the window terrified me. You may be wondering why I'm in a room, hidden? Well, I don't know, as my family never told me. But when it struck 12:00 2 years ago, my sister never hid and she was not seen again. I felt something gently stroking my back...

Erin Hoare (11)
Burford School, Burford

9 Minutes Till Hell

I looked at the clock and there were only 9 minutes till midnight. Time was running out. In precisely 9 minutes, the world as we knew it would end. My hands were shaking, quivering, twitching nervously. All I could hear was the silent ticking of a bomb that would end all of humanity. Time was of the essence, but I felt utterly helpless. There was nothing I could do. I prepared myself for the worst, bracing myself for what was to come. 3, 2, 1... With the click of a finger, all was lost. Everything ever created - gone.

Harvey Thrower (14)
Burford School, Burford

Time Toad

Hello, my friends. What am I? A toad, a time toad. If you're wondering why I am screaming, I will get to that in a moment. I'm sick and tired of people using me for my own power; you see, my power is to stop time. If you live in this world, you'll know people will do anything for a crumb of power. Because of my power, I've been toad-napped 12 times and almost been killed 5 times. Emperors and kings have fought over me. I'm one of the top 10 most wanted 'beasts'. You will never catch me.

Kian Whalley (12)
Burford School, Burford

The 777

It was him. I knew it was him from the day I saw him at the shooting range. I fell for him; his smile, his hair, his humour, his personality. I fell for all of him. The truth is, I didn't even know anything about him other than what he was open about. I needed to find out his name. So I made that my mission for the night. I called it 'Mission: Identity'. It sounds stupid, I know, but when he's all you can think about, it helps distract the mind. A stranger walked past me and said, "777."

Amelia Day-Quilty (12)
Burford School, Burford

Number 19

The ticking grew louder. A sudden rush tingled through my arm. Worried, I looked at my wrist. A number was tattooed on it. 19. An alarm went off, snapping me out of my position. The alarm stopped. Sounds came rushing back. This number, 19, was a number given to me since birth. My number. The number 19 was my identity. I remembered! Suddenly, a mechanical whirring sound came from the white door in front of me. I stared at the door, holding in the sound of a yelp. They'd found me. Numbers 11, 14 and 16. Oh no.

Sama Sadiq (12)
Burford School, Burford

Room 11

Have you ever been to that one place that makes you feel uneasy and unsafe? Well, for me, that's Room 11 of my local apartment block. It all started when I entered for my first overnight stay. It was silent and a strong aroma lurked around the apartment. The smell of horror filled the air. My eyes squinted and my nose twitched.
Suddenly, there I was, lying on the bathroom floor, with no clue what was happening. I shut my eyes tightly and prayed in my sleep as a dark shadow arrived and leaned over me...

Millie Merry (12)
Burford School, Burford

The Bomb

I was on a plane when a scary man screamed, "I have a bomb and in 10 minutes, it'll explode!" I'd never been so scared. He said, "If anyone moves, I will set it off." I wasn't sure what to do. I was a dead man if I stayed there, so I had to try something. I slowly got out of my seat and walked down the aisle until... he saw me. I ran for my life and he screamed, "You're all dead now!"
I made it to the cabin, put on a parachute and jumped out. It then exploded.

Jack Botcherby (13)
Burford School, Burford

The Countdown To Survival

For a moment, time stood still. I could hear the countdown: 5, 4, 3... The sound of the warden's voice rang in my ears. He was shouting at the people who weren't in line. The loudspeakers were announcing the numbers as the clock counted down. My heart was racing and my palms were sweaty. This was the moment I had been training for, this was the moment my mind had been focused on for the past month. 2... I had waited for this. The only thing I had to do was survive. 1... This was when the games began...

Téa Mackie (12)
Burford School, Burford

Patient 22

As I was getting ready for bed, something caught my eye. The digital clock on my bedside table displayed the time: 22:00. I'd seen that number before! Then I thought, *was it the 22nd train platform I was on earlier? Was it the house number I saw earlier? No!* Then I remembered. The crazy asylum patient I had a scary experience with a year ago. Patient 22! That's why I saw 22s. I looked over at the door as soon as I heard a cough. I froze. He was there in my doorway, standing tall. Patient 22!

Imogen Turner (13)
Burford School, Burford

The Bomb

Bang! A loud noise came from downstairs. I put my slippers on and crept down the stairs. I peeked around the corner. I heard ticking. I followed the sound to try and find out what it was. I made my way to the kitchen and looked in all the cupboards. Nothing. I looked in the freezer. Nothing. I looked in the utensil drawer. Nothing. I looked in the fridge and the sound got louder. I saw it. It was a bomb. It had a timer on it. I didn't know what to do. 1:30... 1:00... 0:45... 0:30... I threw it!

Annabelle Rowland (12)
Burford School, Burford

The 10th Chime

The emerald-green hue glistened in the moonlight, blinding the oh-so-tense woman. The Greek antique. An inch away, Big Ben chimed. She dropped down slowly. It ticked once. She nabbed the vase. *Tick.* And made her way slowly onto the cobbled roof. *Tick.* Then she sat catching her breath. *Tick.* The sirens became louder. *Tick.* She jumped. *Tick.* The sirens were deafening. *Tick. Tick. Tick.* It chimed for the 10th and last time. She got away. London fell silent.

Siân Cockett (12)
Burford School, Burford

Number 57

Number 57. That's all I am now. Every time the sound of the clock goes by, it is another human gone. Even the overwhelming screams of their pain are cancelled out by the silence of them waiting, waiting for their number to be called, for them to leave this world. Only 65 left until I'm next. 64, 63... The clock continues to tick as, one by one, the white room turns red and bodies go pale. 58. I close my eyes as a laser points to the number implanted in my chest. I say goodbye to the last tick made.

Georgie Pratley (14)
Burford School, Burford

Escape Room

As I entered the dark and damp room, a crowd of people cheered me and my opponent on. The tense atmosphere frightened me but my opponent showed no emotion. The judge was ready. 3, 2, 1... Go! I listened in closely, hoping to understand how the lock worked. I thought I'd cracked it and entered '526'. But a buzzer sounded around the room, showing it was wrong. My opponent had no luck either. I knew I had to guess quickly. 5 seconds left. 1 more try. I entered '5472'. The door unlocked...

Caiden Barnard (12)
Burford School, Burford

Countdown To Death

103, 102, 101... The countdown had begun. The countdown to my death. My legs started to run. Run for safety, run for help. Was it the end? Or was it the beginning of my new life: the afterlife? Ear-piercing shrieks rolled around my ears and my legs froze. I knew; I knew that was now my fate. The fate of death. 69, 68, 67... I was slowly running out of time... and life. The code started to spin and the room was silent. *Click, click, click*. The door remained shut. It was the end, the end for me...

Isobel Lane (12)
Burford School, Burford

069

Have you ever been framed? As I was walking through the hallways, everyone was giving me 'that' look. When I went over to my locker, it was locked up. The principal called me into their office. I had been framed! Someone had put a bomb in my locker with a timer of 069 hours left on it, but they didn't believe me. They checked CCTV. It turns out someone in a 069 football jersey had done it. However, I still got put into juvenile cell 069. Top floor. I then soon got let out. It was all over...

Thomas Buckland (14)
Burford School, Burford

Mark 3

Number 3 was my number. That's all I was. My life counted on my powers, my mystical powers that were gifted to me. The gods we praised for my powers. But there were 3 of me. Each night, a massacre. One by one, little by little, we all vanished. Gone, all gone. Number 1 was dead with her powers too. Her power was speed, she was as quick as light. 2 and 3 had fire and air but this wasn't blessed on us. It was forced. Chained up, death waiting. Mist flooded in, forming the power that death gave me.

George McCole (12)
Burford School, Burford

World War II: 1939

It was 1939 and war had broken out. I hid in my basement alone. My heart pounded in my chest and my forehead dripped with sweat. I felt as if I was dead; my limbs felt loose and I hadn't eaten for days. I would have rather died of starvation than have them find me. I thought about the life I missed out on and my poor mother. I dug my fingernails into my arm as I heard the loud gunshots and screams of innocent lives being demolished and destroyed. I wished I hadn't been born. Save me from 1939.

Bluebell Evie Stratton (11)
Burford School, Burford

Friday The 14th

It was Friday the 14th, a dark, gloomy day. Nobody was out because of the big outbreak of Chloria Virus. People always wondered why I was outside. Well, it was because I was immune. This meant I couldn't catch it or get ill from it. I was now in what seemed like a good prison. *Who am I?* Well, I couldn't tell you myself because my identity was stolen by the place I was in now. Everyone had a number tattooed on their left wrist. It turns out I had 1, a tattooed number. I was number 14.

Lily-May Gale (12)
Burford School, Burford

The Escape

97, 96... The clock was ticking. The room felt damp and the air was thick. It felt like my throat had closed. I was all alone. There was no object in the room, no escape. I was trapped, stuck. I'd die there. There was a magnetic door keeping me in my empty coffin. It was a room. I worked there and knew the combination, but the lock was on the other side. I grabbed a paperclip out of my pocket. I pulled out the socket and shoved the paperclip behind it. The door then burst open and I had escaped.

Joe Slater (12)
Burford School, Burford

Operation 12

There were 2 secret spy societies. I was part of 1 of them. *Bang!* The box next to me shattered to pieces as I rolled to safety. Shots were being fired. They kept missing. It was my third mission, named Operation 12. This was because my mission was to take down the 12 biggest mafia bosses in France. I had gotten rid of 11, this was the last 1. There was only 1 box left; I had to take my shot. I slid out from behind the box and fired. I hit it. Operation 12 was over. I had won.

Seb Blizzard (13)
Burford School, Burford

Coming Home

18 miles to get there. We turned to street number 14. After a long 304 minutes, we arrived at the beach at 1:27pm. The speed the waves were going was 48mph. The temperature that day was 57°C. That evening, we left to travel back home. It took 30 minutes longer. I was sad to leave and cried for 8 minutes in the car. On the way back, I read 2 whole chapters of my book in the car.
When we got home, the time was 10:52pm. I went to bed and turned 3 lights off. I then fell asleep.

Ella Merry (12)
Burford School, Burford

The Vampire Spy

1 wrong step was fatal. I was on a cliff, surrounded by lava. Death was almost certain. How was I supposed to get out this time? My name's Jose and I'm a vampire. Let me tell you how I go into this mess. I was 12 when I got bitten by a vampire, and I was already a vampire by then. Okay, back to the present. There was a stalactite above me, I used it to swing over. Safe at last! I transformed into a bat and flew past every single guard. I ducked past the fence and got home.

Aaron Self (12)
Burford School, Burford

1 Of Us Was Lying...

There were 2 of us. No one else was there, just us. We didn't know what to do. 1 of us was lying, but which one? I knew I wasn't lying... Hi, I'm number 7 and we're all stuck in these tiny rooms. There is no escape. We were just waiting to be let out. 1 of us was lying. Our friend, Ruby, died. No one knew how it happened. We never got told what happened to her, but she only ever saw 2 people, me and Tianna. I knew the pin to the door, but we couldn't get out...

Leigha Tomkins (12)
Burford School, Burford

World War IIII

Thud! Boom! My heartbeat was in sync with the explosions outside. The bombs went off for 4 minutes before it all stopped; the bombs, my heart. It was like time froze itself, yet I could still move. I walked outside and saw a man with 4,000 credits. If I could kill him, I would be rich. He was clearly a high rank, so this would be hard. Time unfroze and I ran at him. He had a massive energy sword and I only had a dagger. It was all or nothing. I stabbed him in the chest...

Escher Morton (12)
Burford School, Burford

379 Is My Escape

I woke up for the 378th time in the same white room. Every morning, every minute, the only number I could think of was 3-7-9. A bowl of slop, my breakfast, was shoved through the little slit on the door. I sat by the door and waited to hear the footsteps of the guards creep away. I ran to the brick on the wall. I pushed it into the wall and the air vent popped open. I took the cover off and took out the long tube of paper with blueprints and a plan. It was finally time...

Jessica Richards (12)
Burford School, Burford

Number 42

I looked at my wrist, 42 was all I could see. It felt like I'd just got my first tattoo. It hurt so much that I could've cried, but when I thought I was crying, I was not. It felt cold but there were no windows. So how could it be cold? It was pitch-black. I couldn't see anything. *What am I? Who am I? When is it going to be over?* I could not stop thinking about stuff. *Am I seeing things? Am I here right now? Will I ever see my family again?*

Isabella Pratley (12)
Burford School, Burford

The Bomb

15 hours to go. I had just boarded the plane. 14 hours to go. The plane was in the air. There was a delay but I was okay. 10 hours to go. It felt a bit strange. I heard a beeping sound coming from the other side of the plane. A man stood up. He was the source of the beeping. He took off his jacket and he had a bomb. Then more men stood up. There was a gunshot. The pilot was dead. The ticking of the bomb got louder. I braced for impact. *Boom!* Everyone was dead.

Arthur Whitlock (12)
Burford School, Burford

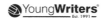

The Ticking Bomb

There was 1 mile left until we got to our mission, but something didn't feel right. When we got to the place, I ran in because I heard a ticking noise. When I entered, I ran straight to the bomb, but an enemy was in the way. So I took him out. I ran to the bomb and started to diffuse it. My hands were shaking and my head was sweating as I finished diffusing the bomb. When I'd finished diffusing it, a sigh of relief rushed over my body as the car sped off.

Stanley Bartle (13)
Burford School, Burford

3am

It was silent besides the occasional *ping* on her phone, but she was awoken by a muffled scream. She went downstairs to see what was going on, but what she saw, she could not believe. There was blood all over the walls and a note saying: 'You're next'. But the second she saw this, she didn't call the police, she just tidied up because she knew what was going to happen next.
The next day, she was reported missing at 3am...

Tienna Dunning Alexander (12)
Burford School, Burford

Just 10 More Days

I looked up at the wall, at the calendar hung on it. Just 10 more days till something happened and I didn't know what. The sound of my heavy breathing and the bead of sweat that just dropped past my tired eyes, caused me to start pacing back and forth. I looked back at the calendar and my eyes drifted to tomorrow's date, the 13th. Marked upon it were the words: 'Death date'. My breathing got heavier and my palms started to sweat...

Lucy Cooper (14)
Burford School, Burford

The Abandoning

It was a dreadful, unwanted day like no other. Tom had hated his life ever since his parents left at the age of 8. Since then, he had been a foster kid, dreaming every day and night about whether he'd ever have a normal life once again. During this tragedy, he gained abilities from the gods below. Ever since he found out about his true powers, his life just switched. Everyone loved him more than before. His emotions were really hitting him...

Alexander Clack (12)
Burford School, Burford

10 Hours To Hell

10 hours to hell. I was excited to finally go to Italy, but when I got there, it was hell. I expected a nice, calm, warm holiday, but instead, it was 48°C and there were weather warnings, so I was only allowed outside for 2 hours a day. This ruined my 1-week holiday. I thought, *why only now has this happened?* The flight home was better than the holiday itself. Everyone was so angry about the heat, but I was just glad it was over.

Oliver Hudson (13)
Burford School, Burford

3 More To Go...

It was waiting to buzz. 6:00, 7:00 and then it went to 8:00. I got up and turned it off but it kept ringing. I didn't know how to stop it, so I threw it on the floor but that didn't help. Then it grew teeth and came at me. I panicked and picked up my baseball bat. But then I saw 5 of them all charging in a row. I dropped the bat. I got the bat and swung at them. I hit 2. I said, "3 more to go!" As I said that, I hit them...

Harry Hudson (12)
Burford School, Burford

11 Seconds To Escape

11 more seconds to go! I was scared. It felt like hours. I sat by a wall in a pool of water. I ran to the bomb and picked it up. I looked at it. 10 more seconds. I kicked it. It went to 9 seconds and started to hiss. I had to snap the wire. 1 would explode it and the other would finally disarm it. Yellow or red? I cut the yellow one. I was right! I was safe. Now, I had to get out. It was going to lock. 5, 4, 3, 2, 1... It was over.

Henry Cooke (12)
Burford School, Burford

The Final Game

It was down to the last 2. The crowd was silent with anticipation, waiting for the final challenge. I looked across at the other player, my mind racing. I needed to win this. The air horn went off, filling the field. Both me and the boy raced to the podium. He was fast, but I was faster. I grabbed the gold token. I won. I looked back as the boy was dragged to his punishment. I'd won, but at what cost?

Somi Ojo (12)
Burford School, Burford

7-Cheetah

7-Cheetah was my code name. It was given to me for my sharp shooting and for being the fastest in the sky. *Slap!* I woke up to shouting and the howling of planes.
"Wake up, Cheetah! We're moving!"
I was unconscious after getting slapped in the face, but could just make out the shape of my F-35 Stealth. My vision found my eyes. My hands shaking, I still managed to take flight...

Charlie Ball (12)
Burford School, Burford

100 Days In A Circle

It's now day 13, 87 days left until I'm free...
14 days ago, I was at home with my family. I went to the park and got kidnapped. I've been forced to stay in this circle for 100 days. Thankfully, they feed me, but it's not enough. I have to do 20 jobs a day. 1 of them is to scam call people to get money for the kidnappers.

Tobias Coombes (12)
Burford School, Burford

Trapped

3 seconds, 2 agents, 1 mission. My legs were trembling with fear as I crept into the vault with Agent Tilly. The room was filled with intense silence as we held our breaths. We climbed through the vault until we made it to the end of the vault. Hands shaking, I cautiously slid the key into the keyhole and unlocked the lock. It was a trap!

Sophie Griffiths (13)
Burford School, Burford

3 Deaths, 2 Murders

Bang! The bullet killed Jack.
"Second murder today, how strange," quivered DI Mooney.
Sheila and Jack now dead, who next? Dr Brown scurried off to find information on the suspects. "Bijingles! Peter Skullivan, known assassin, is on the island. Yesterday, he withdrew a deposit box labelled 'Handgun' by MI5."
They went to find him for questioning.
Hours later, he was found in a house by the sea, 9mm gun in hand. It matched Jack and Sheila's bullets. Blood covered his home. A suicide note was signed beside him: 'I can't continue this life'. In the kitchen lay deposit box 256...

Hedley Windows (15)
Consett Academy, Consett

13: Unlucky For Some

I was number 13. Unlucky, some might say. Better than sleeping rough, others would argue - they'd be wrong.
"94, come with us!" someone bellowed whilst I wallowed in my metal-coated room, gazing into emptiness, regretting, thinking. Every day was a mystery, but what unfolded on the other side of that door, even more so. All I knew: they never came back.
Hours later, making small talk with captors sat around face-down in gruel, I then heard the dreaded... "13! You're up!"
I peered at the man adjacent who sighed in despair before letting out a sorrowful, "Goodbye, son."

Charlotte Lloyd (14)
Consett Academy, Consett

Mystery Of November 5th

It was Bonfire Night; a time for cheer. Everyone gathered around to celebrate. We watched on in awe as vibrant explosions of colour dashed across the skyline. It was incredible until a faint scream could be heard in the distance. Everyone seemed to let it pass over their heads, directing their focus on the display. That was until the screams got closer. Everyone's heads turned. *Bang!* Another scream. Panic spread across the crowd. I felt my heart pounding. One by one, people disappeared around me. I felt something grab me from the shadows. My body became deathly numb. Complete darkness...

Lewis Robson (15)
Consett Academy, Consett

An Empty World At 7am

William opened his drowsy eyes. Alarms rang deafeningly, flashing 7am. School time! "Ugh," he groaned. William was a reserved boy, aged 10, who lived with his brother, his sister and their loving parents. William lived and breathed karate. This, we all knew. Climbing down the stairs, the silence filled his little heart with fear. The door was left open. There was nobody home. Panic-stricken, he ran to find the phone; dialling and ringing. Voicemail.
It was hours later, the sun set and there was still an empty world. William clambered into bed, begging for his family to come home.

Ellen Jewson (15)
Consett Academy, Consett

13, The Unlucky Or Lucky Number?

13... A very misunderstood number - like the boy who cried wolf. James bought 12 lottery tickets every night. Eventually, after 4 long years, the numbers for the £1 billion pound prize were drawn. All identical... 1 number to go. His heart was racing like an F1 car's engine. T-th-thirteen. James had won. He was a billionaire, but how? 13's unlucky, or is it? James left the money in his house.
One night, he heard the window of his newly-bought mansion smash. 3 masked and armed men rushed in with AK-47s and other dangerous weaponry. *Bang! Bang! Bang!* Was he alive?

Georgie Eglon (12)
Consett Academy, Consett

Going Back In Time

3:20pm, 2/3/23:
It's a cold, rainy day and my life is boring. What did the people in the past do to pass time?
3:32pm, 2/3/23:
I'm surrounded by ginormous buildings which look ancient, one with 1903 engraved. I wonder what life was like then?
3:33pm, 2/3/1903:
For a split second, I blink. The date has changed on my watch. It's 1903. The tall buildings look almost new and the air is grey with thick smoke. Have I time-travelled? Cars that were parked up are now horses and carts and the concrete roads are now cobbled streets.

Nona Richardson (14)
Consett Academy, Consett

The Countdown

I questioned how I managed to end up in this... place? 10, I felt my heart pounding, ripping out of my chest. 9, rain trickled mercilessly down my flushed face. 8, the trees outside screamed and shrieked in the howling rain. 7, my throat slowly closed up, not even a whisper could escape this hell. 6, 5, my mind raced at light speed. "4, 3!" the voice shouted. 2, I became hyper-aware of my breathing. It was shaking, making me breathless. 1! "Your time's up!"
I blacked out and found myself somewhere unfamiliar.
How will I ever escape this loop?

Safia Mitchell (12)
Consett Academy, Consett

Project 453

Shoulders tense. No one dares to breathe. The clock ticks painfully. One number yet to be drawn. Muffled screams and flailing arms come from the chosen being dragged away. Echoes of footsteps break the silence. The click of a key, about to seal someone's fate. Everyone's heads dart down as a booming voice speaks, "Finally, project 453." It can't be... I look at the embroidery in disbelief. 453. Strong arms haul me away and bound me to a locked room. Before I can move, a glinting needle impales my arm. Excruciating pain floods my veins as my eyes flutter shut...

Holly Sant (13)
Consett Academy, Consett

Alien Investigation #1588

Walking through my office, I flick through the evidence on case 1588. Could aliens be real? A file that is labelled 'Evidence number 16' catches my eye. This file was photo evidence displaying a green substance oozing through the drains. We had witnesses of this, however, they saw them indirectly. Witness 11 stated: "I looked into my mirror and saw the flash of a flying object through my window." I'm unsure about this case. I'm a scientist trained to look at facts. But right now, there are no facts for or against aliens. But, do you believe in aliens?

Mia Emery (14)
Consett Academy, Consett

The Final 10

I woke up. The springy mattress felt as hard as a rock. As I forced my eyes open, I saw at least 100 people in the same situation as me - lost and confused. In a windowless room, speakers blared out, "Be quiet! 90 will die, 10 will survive!" There were murmurs until a chain of explosions. *Bang! Bang! Bang!* At least 50 people died. I stood stunned, frozen in fear. There was a scream. *Bang!* Talking. *Bang!* More screaming. *Bang!* The speakers blared out music and the voice said, "Well done! You are in the final 10 people!"

Flynn Thompson (13)
Consett Academy, Consett

7th Heaven

Newcastle United were beating Sunderland 7-0 and there were only 7 minutes left. Number 7 was Newcastle's new striker and he had scored all 7 goals. This was a massive game. If the score remained the same, which was highly probable, Newcastle would finish 7th in the championship. This would be their best finish in the 7-year history of the competition. Newcastle were counting down the minutes until the end of the game. There would be major celebrations throughout the city. There were 7 seconds left and number 7 was poorly challenged. This was a massively big disaster.

Daniel Ashurst (13)
Consett Academy, Consett

The Washington Heist

Washington State Bank: owned by the most pompous hoarders in the US. We'd be the ones to take it down. Hoxton's plan was to enter the bank, drill into the vault, get the money and leave as few casualties as possible. Simple. We got out of the van. Duke decided to bring a minigun and a thermal drill. This would be a breeze.
"I'll wait in the van, you go," Hoxton called from the van.
We entered, guns blazing and went straight to the vault. We were in. First box I opened, 482, a small device flashed.
"Run!" It detonated...

Alexander Charlton (13)
Consett Academy, Consett

A Prison Escape

Prisoner 21: missing? Last night, a prisoner escaped from the mighty jail of Middlesbrough. He had black hair, brown eyes, and was estimated to be 6'4'' tall. His escape was made at around 1:24am in the morning whilst the police officers were sleeping and his jail mates were zoned out. Officers say he managed to dig out a massive hole in the wall leading to the barbed wire fences, which he climbed over by using a ladder. Police helicopters had been searching the streets for 3 hours now, but hadn't spotted prisoner 21. The police wouldn't give up!

Matthew Clemitson (12)
Consett Academy, Consett

Room 13

Stumbling down the ancient, wooden hallway, she left behind a muddy footprint. Unstable floorboards made a high-pitched squeak as she set her boot onto it. Then it all went silent... The abused door towered over her whilst she stood there, frozen. Slowly, she placed her warm hand on the ice-cold doorknob. Trembling in fear, she twisted it and the door flew open... almost as if someone snatched it away from her. Darkness devoured Room 13, the only light was the sudden flash of lightning. Unexpectedly, the door slammed behind her. It refused to open. She was trapped.

Isobella Heenan (12)
Consett Academy, Consett

Batman's Conundrum

Batman was checking his digital database. He was searching for a cure for the Joker as he'd taken a drug that made him more insane! He finally found it. Conundrum 472. It matched the DNA of the Joker. Now, he was ready. Courageously, Batman jumped into his Batmobile at the speed of light and prepared his engine. He searched the streets, looking for Joker, tracking his last known location. At last, Batman found him. He raced into battle, but Joker blocked him. Suddenly, Robin swooped in and held Joker down. Batman grabbed the cure and used in on the Joker.

Kai Storey (12)
Consett Academy, Consett

13 Months

Nervously, we hurried down the grey, rocky path until we almost collapsed. It was the 13th of October and the moon lit up the forest like a stage, seeming to get bigger. Wind whistled around us and the tall, shadowed, surrounding trees loomed over us. Thinking we'd lost it, 3 of us lay under the bright stars watching over us. Nobody was even trying to find us. We'd been gone for 13 months, searching. We'd found it. Although it was extremely underwhelming; 13 months we'd been trying to find the heirloom and it was all a lie. We'd given up.

Natalie Ward (14)
Consett Academy, Consett

My Golden Birthday

It's my golden birthday. I'm turning 10 on the 10th of October 2010. I went to school just like normal and I was sat in English when the fire alarm went off. It was an armed intruder. I sprang off my seat and ran to the nearest closet. My heart thumped so hard, I could feel it in my ears. I sat there silently wondering why the cacophony of screams had fallen silent. Suddenly, the door creaked open. A man, unidentifiable, was revealed. He clasped a golden knife.
"Happy birthday, little girl," he said deeply.
Everything went black.

Mollie Walls (15)
Consett Academy, Consett

1438 Aventis Way

1438 Aventis Way, the house that made me leave Texas and never come back. It was February 2011; the metallic rattle of keys turning in the door. All seemed well, perfect even. For days, I envisioned the potential to make this dated bungalow my home. The impossible task began a swift week later. The strange mismatch on the floor. I thought splinters would be my worst enemy. A dangerous mistake. Days went by, a plastic tub was uncovered. Taking a glance inside, the glint of knives, stained deep red with blood. Sirens soon followed on Friday the 13th of March.

Charlie Wright (14)
Consett Academy, Consett

End Of The Line

It was 2999... With 2,999 seconds left until 3000. My breaths came as the pain in my chest seared. What was happening? I staggered over to the control panel. Less than 10% oxygen left. I was the last 1 alive. The robots had taken over. The scientists were wrong. We had not survived. 1,000 seconds left. I fell to my knees. *So this is what dying feels like? Interesting...* 2% oxygen left. 500 seconds left. My vision started to fade. 1% oxygen. 100 seconds. *I might live to the next year*. Well, goodbye Earth. Darkness overpowered me.

Grace Morris (11)
Consett Academy, Consett

Only 1 Way Out

18 was small and roughly carved out. 18... Only a few days ago, I had been training endlessly for this. I was determined that nothing would stop me but this, this door. It dragged me in, step by step. Each step I took, the more my stomach dropped; alarm bells rang louder. Tiny yet so powerful, the engraved 18 burned into my eyes, beckoning me. I reached out and turned the handle. I stepped into the darkness, running my fingertips along the symbols. I was locked in.
A voice loudly boomed, "There is only 1 way out of here: Escape!"

Jaya Saundh (12)
Consett Academy, Consett

Always Number 2

I stood there as Marceline once again received praise for her perfect score on the test, only 1 mark above mine. She was always the best. I was always number 2. I sighed and began walking home. I made my way towards the dreary back alleys, polar opposites to Marceline's gorgeous mini-mansion. Then the rain came. I put up my umbrella but it was just swept away by the beastly winds. I stood there, on the brink of crying, rain dripping onto my hair and glum, morose face. However, I noticed a little bottle wash up near my feet. Poison.

Lily-Jennifer Newman (13)
Consett Academy, Consett

Friday The 13th

It was Friday the 13th and me and my friend Akadn decided to go into an abandoned building. When we entered, we saw something suspicious. We saw the shadow of an old, creepy, terrifying man. We didn't think about it that much until the end of the night. The clock struck midnight and we heard a loud, mysterious noise saying, "Get out of my pub now, you meddling kids!" We didn't know if it was a trick or real life. We panicked, not knowing what it was. We ran out of the building without any regrets and the night ended.

Anya Curry (15)
Consett Academy, Consett

60 Seconds

60 seconds left. Water surrounds me like Monday morning mist. I struggle for air but it gets harder every time. I flail my arms, light from the surface peeking through. I've stopped trying to fight now, I'm too weak for that. Numb to the cold, I know time is running out. All of my instincts scream at me to swim, but I don't. Serenity washes over me, I'm no longer afraid. Is this what death feels like? My body grows limp as the world becomes nothing more than a blur of colour. My time is up now. 60 seconds gone.

Kayla-Marie Atkinson (12)
Consett Academy, Consett

The Last 24 Hours

With 23 hours and 54 minutes left, everyone was going crazy. Everyone wanted to know what would happen when the timer ended. The countdown was in the air. It started on a rainy day, but as the sun started to shine, you could start to see the hologram in the air. There were 23 hours left. People started going crazy. They tried driving away but a hologram with a timer followed them. Rich people got into jets, but when they got to a certain point, their plane blew up. The timer was at 00:00:02. No! *Bang!* The world ended.

Noah Deelen (12)
Consett Academy, Consett

Dragon 56

Quickly, I ran home to 10 Ivy Lane, ready to make my choice. Removing the dangers from my mind, I selected to battle a dragon. It seemed as if time stood still. Eventually, when the task began, a dragon labelled 56 emerged from a cave. The dragon glared at me with its royal blue scales and amber eyes before shooting scorching hot flames inches away from me. I froze in fear before I reached to grab the closest sharp object hoping to slay the dragon. I charged at the dragon with all my strength. I had slain the ferocious dragon.

Katie Simm (13)
Consett Academy, Consett

She Should Never Have Eaten The Cake

16 candles to mark her 16th birthday, the day she had desired for years. The cake's divine-looking chocolate and vibrant pink icing drew her and made her want to take a sneaky bite. But before she could, her mum came into the family kitchen to light the candles. The lighter refused to light, but eventually, they managed. The sparks flickered and sparked everywhere like a warning sign. As soon as she took a bite, lime-green liquid ran out of the cake and she dropped dead. Poison. She died that day and will forever be 16.

Leighel Calvert (12)
Consett Academy, Consett

Code Jail

Running as fast as I could, I suddenly turned a sharp corner. 1, 2, 3 security guards were chasing me. Why? I shut down the lasers protecting the diamond gem. It was easy to find out the code. 4-3-2-1 was so incredibly easy - next time, change it. *Ow!* I tripped over my shoelace and landed on my face, flat against the gravel ground. I knew it was over. I was going to live my life in jail. "You're screwed, kid."
As I was taken away in the van, I said my lucky number in my head again: *100*.

Hannah Thompson (12)
Consett Academy, Consett

I Am Number 13

I am number 13. Everywhere I go, I see number 13. It's constantly in my head, reminding me of the pain I have caused. I see it on computer screens, it is everywhere. Every Friday the 13th, I do something terrible. Nobody knows it's me that causes it, nobody will ever know. Every Friday the 13th, I am responsible for someone's death - no matter how hard I try not to be. Everyone says Friday the 13th is an unlucky day. But to me, it's a deadly day. This time though, I'll be the 1 dying on Friday the 13th.

Amy Forbes (13)
Consett Academy, Consett

A Second Chance

I was in school, as usual, in English writing a story for a competition. There was a deafening silence. All of a sudden, extremely loud bangs came from the ground floor. An alarm went off. I was scared. The teacher commanded us to get under our desks. I was the 1 next to the door. Suddenly, the door swung open. My heart sank. He had a revolver in his hand. My instinct was to attack him and I did. I knocked him out and grabbed the gun. 1 bullet in the chamber. I saw the other shooter and *bang!* ..."Hello?"

Noah Orrick (12)
Consett Academy, Consett

The 1st: April Fools

It was April 1st, I thought it would be a hilarious day... It wasn't. Rain was pattering on my window. I opened my eyes and saw a dark figure. It happened so quickly, like the speed of light. I opened my eyes. It was a basement. It smelt like expired milk. There was May, why did she kidnap me? "April Fools!" she shouted. What. The. Why did she do this? It was because of April Fools. I wanted to scream but decided against it. I could hear the wind howling. It had been a week. I was out! Thank goodness.

Mieke Verheij-Cousins (12)
Consett Academy, Consett

50 Doors...

1... I'm at door 1. How am I meant to make it to door 50? *Creak!* I open the door. This room is massive. Where could the door be?
10 minutes later, I'm only at door 8. Great! OMG! There's a creature! It's trying to kill me! I need to get out of here! Phew! I make it out. Thank god!
2 hours and many creatures later, door 49 is standing right in front of me. I can't believe I actually did it. As I open the door, a sigh of relief exits my body. Oh, wait! There's another door...

Ava Jackson (12)
Consett Academy, Consett

3

Slam! Locker number 3 slams shut, nearly catching my face!
I climb into the car, Radio 3 blares through my ears. Looking out the window, 3 pops up everywhere. *Am I going crazy?*
That night, my heart skips a beat when my alarm wakes me at 3 in the morning. Why at 3?
The next morning, I scamper into the car. My eyes struggle to stay open. It's the 3rd of March 2023. I look ahead to see a monster of a lorry with a giant '3' on the front. It's out of control. Then... Darkness.

Eleanor Raeburn (15)
Consett Academy, Consett

The Monster In Room 242

I sat all alone, shivering. I was in the cursed room of 242. There had been many disappearances within these four walls (my sister being one of the many). There was a signal to mark its presence... The lights went out, but once they came on, one student was missing. I sat twiddling my thumbs until... the class was in darkness! I felt a crooked claw caress my foot, so I looked down towards it. It looked like a swirling black mist with piercing ruby eyes. I went to scream but it was too late. The demon bit my neck...

Kaye-Grace Parkin (12)
Consett Academy, Consett

Ready, Player 9?

My eyes slowly shut and it all went black. My hands clenched the soft duvet that was draped over me. A faint buzzing noise filled my ears. I woke up to see what it was. *Am I still in the dream?* No. This was too real. I was unfamiliar with my surroundings. I dropped my focus to my hand. 9. In black marker, the number 9. I was in my own bed, but what surrounded me wasn't the same. I was confused by what was happening to me. Then, all of a sudden, a voice said loudly, "Ready, player 9?"

Vanessa Bourn (13)
Consett Academy, Consett

Room 101

Cautiously, I crept up to the room. 101. The scene of the crime. I had to know what happened there, however uneasy it might be. The door creaked open. I needed more answers. As I made my way through the apartment, I came across something I was not ready for. A stream of fresh, warm, flowing blood. I did the one thing I shouldn't have, I followed it. It led me to the bathroom and once I entered, I had my answer. The killer lay there on the floor, his head oozing with blood; a gun in his hand.

Jack Byrne (14)
Consett Academy, Consett

5 Footsteps

It was a cold winter morning and when I opened my door to leave my home, I stopped in my tracks. As I looked down at the ground in front of me, I saw 5 footprints in the snow. They looked fresh and everyone else in my family hadn't left the house yet. I couldn't take my eyes off them - they weren't disappearing despite the fact it was snowing heavily. However, I would be late if I didn't go soon, and as I walked, my feet matched up with them. 1, 2, 3, 4, 5... And then I was gone.

Sophie McClen (14)
Consett Academy, Consett

The Numbered Murderer

I went to sleep on Thursday and when I woke up on Friday the 13th of November 2018, I was in a mysterious place. There were about another 11 people. They were all numbered up to 11, another person was 12, and I was 13. An announcer spoke: "1 of you is a murderer and has a knife. The rest of you need to find out who they are and the sheriff must shoot them. Good luck!" Someone died. Number 5 found 7 dead. Everyone disclosed their location before it was reported. 1 of us was lying...

Scott Franklin (14)
Consett Academy, Consett

The Camp

Who? Who could be so cruel? The case was absolutely horrid. Someone had abducted a whole camp of teenage girls. We were too scared to go into the cabin, so we looked in through the window. Oh no! There were the remains of the girls... *Oh, god! There were whole bodies!* We went and took a closer look and each girl had 15 seconds engraved on their wrists. We looked around and found a blood trail leading to the bathroom, where we found the camp leader... covered in... *blood!*

Sophie Cromar (11)
Consett Academy, Consett

The Prison Escape

I woke up on my 31st day in prison. The weather was hurricane-like, but I couldn't see it. There was no window in sight, except a minuscule light bulb. I knew I had to escape! The guards' shifts were easy to memorise. I knew I had 31 seconds to get out. The time had come. It was 1:31am. I had a good idea of the code. Then my heart leapt up into my throat as I entered the 6-digit code: '310131'. Then I heard a sudden crash on the hard stone floor. I was free!

Isabelle Bone (12)
Consett Academy, Consett

Number 13

I was chosen out of 1,600 people. Me and 99 others were picked for the bingo game. I was sweating but then I got my number. 13. *Yup! I'm dead! Tomorrow will be my death day.* 2:37am, I couldn't sleep knowing today was potentially the day of my death... As I arrived, I watched everybody's parents say their goodbyes. God, bless me. I walked through door 237, the room of death. Numbers after numbers, and now it was me and number 66. God, bless me.

Lauren Taylor (12)
Consett Academy, Consett

The Fall

Back breaking, bones aching, I climbed the hill the killer told me to. My heart was pounding and I was sweating so much. I saw a light in the distance. 1 minute to get there, 1 minute to save my life. *It's 4:43, I better run.* Panting, I made it up the hill. The mud was slippery, but he was there, holding up my money. 30 seconds. Running as fast as I could, my shoe fell off and I slipped. *Click.* It was a landmine. *Don't move...*

Isla Upton (11)
Consett Academy, Consett

What's Inside The Bag?

There was 1 mile to go on the journey to find the missing child. We received a call from the parents. They said, "The last we saw our boy, he was in the woods." So we went to the woods to try and find any clues. Suddenly, we found a bag with a rain jacket inside. We found a name in the bag and the name was James. I investigated the wet raincoat and there was also a baseball cap with a photo inside the cap. We looked inside the cap and we saw...

Mason Wray (14)
Consett Academy, Consett

Cart Crash

The competition began. This was the final day of the competition. It was even, 8-8. 4 more holes left. The golfers both went for their swing (not at the same time) and both got a hole-in-one. 9-9. As they went to the final hole... *Crash!* One of the golfers hit something metal. The other golfer started to laugh. The other one tried to pick it up and chuck it. They started to dig frantically. What was it?

Logan Hannant-Thompson (12)
Consett Academy, Consett

The Time Traveller

It was 1985 and I was driving my car. I was going 87mph, but as I reached 88mph, I went into space. How could this happen? I was being dragged back down to Earth at mind-blowing speeds. As I got closer and closer, it looked different. The cars were flying, but this was impossible. *Will I ever get back? But how?* My car was broken. Then I saw my car was on fire. This was the end...

Robert Liddle (12)
Consett Academy, Consett

15 Seconds To Live

Everyone in the country knew my name. I remember when the clamouring journalists became like my shadow, following me everywhere. Those days are gone. Claws pin me to the ground, yet my head lifts, searching for an escape. Their cave lies thousands of feet beneath Mars' cratered surface. I'm beyond help. Suddenly, a heavy blow hits the back of my head. My eyes boil and burn; I make out my helmet in front of me, but I'm grappling blindly. A familiar voice echoes around my head: "If you lose your helmet, you've got 15 seconds to live."

Zoe Capon (12)
Longdean School, Bennetts End

Judgement Day

10, I sprinted across the cold, hard marble floor barefooted, my wounds on each side of my stomach feeling like 10,000 bullets hitting my sides every second. 9, it was all up to me to stop the computer virus destined to implode the Earth. 8, despite the fact that my legs felt like goo, I was still running exponentially fast. 7, 6, 5, I had a feeling I was going to make it! 4, 3, I accidentally tripped over my legs. I couldn't get up! We were doomed! 2, I shut my eyes, waiting for death. 1, *annihilation!*

Amir Abderrakib (14)
Longdean School, Bennetts End

The Fallen

Destroyed, I crashed to the ground. I burned. Was I ever 1 of them? I shone but was I ever one of them? Always an outsider, ostracised. Abandoned by my sisters. Yet I remained whole, I was home. The only place I had ever known, couldn't that be called home? Watching the world below. I yearned to see it up close but I could only do so for so long before it became my obsession and I fell into despair. 1,000,000,000 years. After all those years, I didn't expect to be shot straight out of the sky...

Keira Langley (15)
Longdean School, Bennetts End

1 Minute Left...

1 minute left. That's all I see. The atmosphere around me goes cold and dark.
"55, 54, 53..."
I try to scream. Nobody, nobody at all.
"Help! Help me!"
I see a big, glass window. Everything's a blur. I can taste the breezy air. I can feel my hair standing on end. I can hear the clock.
"25, 24, 23..."
"What is this? Where am I? Can anybody hear me?"
"10, 9, 8..."
I start feeling weak.
"Somebody, help!"
I try to run to the window and something grabs me from behind.
"3, 2, 1..."
I start to fall. *Boom!*

Zainab Ajmal (13)
Madni Academy, Savile Town

Run Away!

There it was. The bloody appearance of my nightmare. Its voice haunted me, I was going insane.
"Number 1. Number 1," it called out.
My body wouldn't move, I felt paralysed. All I could focus on was the demented number '1', from its crusty, cracked face to its inner stench. It came to me again.
"Go away!" I screamed.
"Number 1 will be in your life forever. Number 1 will conquer you. Number 1 will take you back to your past."
I wanted to run away somewhere so it couldn't find me. I wanted to be free and live life!

Humaira Nana (12)
Madni Academy, Savile Town

We'll Never Know

He said he'd meet me there. Row 187. I walked into the dark, gloomy library and in the corner I saw a petite, old woman, her glasses halfway down her nose. I showed her the note with the book's name.
She stared at it with a strange, startled look before looking up and replying, "Row 187."
I strolled around, stroking my hands across the books as I walked down the rows and rows of shelves. I'd been walking around for half an hour when finally, at the end, I found it: row 187. Suddenly, something grabbed me from behind...
"Argh!"

Khadeejah Salam (12)
Madni Academy, Savile Town

How'd I Get Here?

It was 12:42pm. This was it, I knew what had to be done. Bus 273 was coming by. I stepped towards the curb to get the driver's attention as he decelerated. The bottom had a large number of people, so I dragged my feet up the stairs. Suddenly, steam suffocated the bus. Shrieking and screams deafened me as I felt as though we fell from the sky. My heart was hammering, I was trembling. I got up instantly, where was I? My head flooded with numerous questions until a nurse came in.
"She woke up! Our 3rd survivor so far..."

Zinab Harim (13)
Madni Academy, Savile Town

The Legend Of 93

This was it. The final moment of truth. I stood there shaking like a leaf. My hand trembled as I reached for the doorknob. The room that had spread terror throughout the village. The door numbered 93 that sent cold shivers down every villager's spine. Was it true? Or was it just a legend? What really lay beyond this door? I slowly turned the doorknob. 93 flickered like a blazing fire. Cold air wooshed and circled around me. My eyes widened with fear. My heart pounded like a wild drum. The horrific legend of door 93 was true...

Haadiyah Hashmi (13)
Madni Academy, Savile Town

1 Mile To Go

There was 1 mile to go and I was already exhausted. I had been travelling since the later part of the night and now, as the sun stealthily rose above the mountain peaks, I sank down to boost my energy. Thinking of the leather skin bag I had filled with water, I took it out and proceeded to drink from it. Thunder rumbled in the distance and lightning struck a nearby cactus. I dropped the water, its remainder spilling onto the golden sands of the desert. Suddenly, I felt the cold metal of a pistol pressed against my clammy neck...

Zainab Raja (12)
Madni Academy, Savile Town

Friday The 13th It Was

Friday the 13th it was. My unlucky day. 1st thing, I woke up late. Then I tripped down the stairs on the way to the bathroom, 13 steps. Suddenly, my mum was calling out to me.

"Get here right now, you have 13 buckets of laundry to do."

I sighed in pain. It was horrific! My head started spinning 13 times in the washing machine. I tasted the soapiness. It was bubbling out of my mouth. I could hear the tumbling and the swishing. I opened my eyes and water started to seep through. 13 is my unlucky number.

Safa Noor (13)

Madni Academy, Savile Town

1 And Only 1...

I could feel the sweat dribbling down my head. Every 1 of us stood still, glaring at the floor. No one bothered moving, talking or even breathing. My heart thumped loudly like a drum. All of a sudden, the door creaked open. A large shadow grew over us. I was traumatised. The lights began to flicker and each time it went dark there was 1 scream. My legs turned to jelly. I tried to run, but I was so horrified by what I saw. The light turned off once again. No one screamed.
All I heard was, "1, 1, 1..."

Maryam Ahmed (12)
Madni Academy, Savile Town

The Friday To Remember

It was Friday the 13th, I couldn't believe my eyes, there was no way the day started again. Let me explain, Friday the 13th's my birthday but this year it went completely wrong. I woke up in the morning to a horrible breakout which made me so upset. Why, on my special day? Then I went downstairs only to find out my family forgot about my birthday. I ignored it, hoping it was a prank. It wasn't. I went upstairs to call my bestie only to find out she was in a coma. I cried and wished that day restarted...

Aisha Bright (14)
Madni Academy, Savile Town

1 Of Us Was Lying...

One day I came back from school, hot and sweaty. I lay there on my bed. I could feel my blood getting clogged up in my body, and my veins tightened. You'll never guess what happened today. My 2 friends, Clara and Sierra, and I were going to music class. All of a sudden, we heard a scream. It was coming from the cloakroom. As Sierra opened the door, she saw Noah lying there. He had a lighter in his hand. Just then, Mr Carter opened the door and we were sent to the head teacher's spooky office...

Umaymah Saleem (13)
Madni Academy, Savile Town

The Fire In Room 5

The alarm goes off. I blink to adjust my eyes. The crimson light flashes. It's 5 minutes until midnight. The fuming flames lick the sign, 5, on the wooden door. I panic as the intense heat pierces my face. I sprint towards the 5th window and cry for help. No answer. My heart gallops as a piece of the fire-eaten ceiling crashes to the floor. I scan the room to find safety. But it's too late to do anything now. I am just an unlucky number. Trapped in room 5.

Aasiya Khan (13)
Madni Academy, Savile Town

The Game

I'm number 13. I'm here in Room 130. I'm 1 of the last people in the game. Tomorrow, we complete another challenge. The last person to complete the challenge will be eliminated. It started with 100 players. There are 10 challenges. They get harder every day, so I'm really lucky to get to this stage. I've made friends here; I've also watched many die. I only have Betty left. The game today is called 'Speak Never'. Nobody can talk anymore until the challenge is over. Hopefully, it's soon. I'm going to tell Betty, "I'm so sorry for what happens tomorrow."

Mollie Beer (13)
Ysgol Bryn Alyn, Gwersyllt

Room 20

"So, is this it? Room 20, the one you said had squealing coming from the other side of the door?" asked Jim.
"Yes," came the shaky reply.
"Well, what are you waiting for? Go on, open it," said Jim.
"Um, okay," came the shaky voice.
But before anyone could touch the handle, it opened by itself. It was pitch-black and smelt like cigarettes. The air was musty. Then Jim and his friend stepped inside. The door suddenly locked behind them with a bang and then a click. This was it. Would they ever come out alive?

Dafydd Sutton (12)
Ysgol Bryn Alyn, Gwersyllt

The Great Hoarders' Hunt

The time struck zero. The time had come. The Hoarders' Hunt had begun. 4 weeks, 4 answers, all hidden in a toddler's puzzle. They were hidden in cyphers, colour codes, comics and piles of gold. One by one, the answers were found: Outc45t, 2faced, 3gdurg and finally, Bait Trap Break Retake. All pointing to the Hoarder that signed with H. His puzzles were meddled with by those he didn't want to take part. A chest opened with a broken curse that killed. With many alive and the Hoarder unpleased, a letter gave his final plea. The end was signed, Hogarth.

Rhys Broderick (15)
Ysgol Bryn Alyn, Gwersyllt

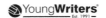

What Happened At House 64?

The night it happened, I would never forget. Stranded there, stranded in the woods, waiting for freedom, for my time! 7am, no one to help me, no one to save me. House 64. It had this haunted type of look that would've made a mummy scream too. I walked up to this so-called house of horror. Blood dripped, screams tortured my brain, and children's laughter hung in the air. "Hahaha!" The door flung open. When I went to grab it, the house suddenly spoke, "Death will strike upon you." These were the very last words I heard till death...

Ava Davies (13)
Ysgol Bryn Alyn, Gwersyllt

The Unlucky 7

Room 777, such a nice suite. My honeymoon was amazing until it wasn't. It was 7am and I woke up startled from an ear-piercing scream. It was my wife. She'd been brutally murdered by her evil ex. I broke down in tears. I cried for 7 hours straight. 7! 7 horrendous hours of crying, without my gorgeous wife. Eventually, I screamed for help. The police arrived soon after with the paramedics. The police investigated for a while and came to a conclusion, the wrong conclusion. They arrested me for the murder of my darling wife! I mean, how unbelievable!

Kara Burton (12) & Evie-Mai
Ysgol Bryn Alyn, Gwersyllt

The Monster By Locker 876

Locker 876. That was where *it* was, the thing that'd followed me throughout my life. That thing, that monster was just standing there staring at me. I felt like if I moved just a slight bit that monster would pounce at me. Locker 876 was my locker and I had to get there because it contained something very important that I couldn't leave behind, no matter what. Whilst thinking about what to do, I looked over to the locker and it wasn't there. A cold shiver went down my spine and I started dripping in sweat. Locker 876 wasn't safe!

Harry Scott (15)
Ysgol Bryn Alyn, Gwersyllt

1 Of Us Was Lying

April 17th, my housewarming party, only a small gathering. 1 or 2 friends came. My friends, Summer, Bethan, and Elizabeth, made a cake. It looked amazing. People passed by the creation complimenting it. After the BBQ, we decided it would be a good time to cut the cake and have a disco. Suddenly, my sister and brother became delusional and collapsed. We called the police and they arrived 15 minutes later. Everyone was interrogated. The party was stopped. We were all taken into different rooms, 1 by 1. They were finished and found out 1 of us was lying.

Willow Jacobs (15)
Ysgol Bryn Alyn, Gwersyllt

72 Isn't Just A Number

72 isn't just a number. It's my grandpa's age. His 72nd birthday was unforgettable. It was the day I visited Grandpa, the day that changed my life. Grandpa greeted me with lemonade on his doorstep. And not even 24 hours later, I was accelerating my legs to run away from the horrors of Grandpa and his shotgun. I was asking myself, *why?* But nobody knew the answer, except Grandma. But Grandma was gone, missing, the only one with the knowledge of Grandpa's true identity. And I was scared that I might be next...

Phoebe Poole (15)
Ysgol Bryn Alyn, Gwersyllt

The Coma

I woke up from the coma I'd been in for many years. I turned to go look at the clock. It flashed the exact time I fell into a coma. The calendar seemed to be the only untouched thing, saying '2099'. The hospital was overgrown, grey and abandoned. This place was mystical. I headed to the elevator, making my way to floor 0. All of a sudden, *thud!* All the numbers were glitching. The door finally opened. 'Level 59, floor 99'. A dice. I picked it up. I rolled a 3. Suddenly, I woke up. It was just a dream.

Eileen Zhang (13)
Ysgol Bryn Alyn, Gwersyllt

The Old Hospital

We began to take a walk down to the edge of town. Me and my friend, Alice, had had a long last week of the year, but it was finally over for the summer. Me and Alice were walking down a path, dimly lit by flickering lamp posts (probably built in 1950!). Suddenly, as we walked past the old hospital, a loud banging noise came from inside; even though nobody had been inside since the accident; or outside. We entered, the door shutting behind us. The room we had heard the noise from shuddered. Above the door read: 'Get out'.

Lilly-Belle Bush (13)
Ysgol Bryn Alyn, Gwersyllt

The Chase Is On

There was 1 mile to go. The time travelling machine aka the TARDIS had a few minutes before it disappeared from existence. We knew that we wouldn't make it in time, but Jeremy, my best mate, didn't give up. He slammed his foot on the pedal of the Dodge Challenger. As we increased the speed of the car, it felt like everything went past us at the speed of sound, and before we knew it, we were there, beside the TARDIS. We sprinted inside the TARDIS, and as we entered it, we felt like the Earth had disappeared beneath us...

Harry Scott (15)
Ysgol Bryn Alyn, Gwersyllt

27 Days

All I have are 27 days. 27 measly days to find this missing child. 'She only went to her grandpa's house' is the worst lie I've ever been told. I know something more sinister is going on here. The question is: what? What happened to that child while she was staying with *him?* He is the answer to all of my questions and I know he has all of the answers that I need to find her. He's behind all of this, but I've only got a laughable 27 days to find her. He'll pay, I'll make sure of it.

Emma Smith (15)
Ysgol Bryn Alyn, Gwersyllt

How I Lost Everything In Vegas

I entered the casino, $100 to my name. If I wanted to get home, I needed to win big. Las Vegas was where it happened. I could only buy 1 chip. That's all I needed. An ace; a king. 21. I won and doubled my money. Blackjack was probably the safest thing to bet on. I kept winning and winning. They kicked me off Blackjack, thought I was counting cards. It didn't matter, I felt lucky. If I kept going, I'd be rich. I went all in. "26 black," I said.
The roulette table spun. 27 red. I lost everything.

Matthew Jones (13)
Ysgol Bryn Alyn, Gwersyllt

The Things We Do For Money

The announcement happened at midday. I had won £1 million pounds on the lottery. Sure, it might have been a coincidence that I had an empty bank account before, but I had done nothing wrong. I did what I had to do to ensure that my family would survive. You might think it was selfish and many called me a traitor, but I was victorious. The question was, how was I going to explain to my parents about what I did? Surely they would understand why.
It all started in the summer when I found locker 876 in my home...

Abigail Watts (15)
Ysgol Bryn Alyn, Gwersyllt

The Last Road Trip

I remember last year, the adventures I went on with my friends. But there is 1 adventure I'll never forget.
It was about 5 years ago when me and my friends went on a road trip to a place called The World's End. It was said that everyone who visited never returned. We drove across the cliffs as the wind howled at us and the birds stopped singing. There was a cave; a deep, dark cave. I felt uneasy but my eager friends went into the cave, hoping to find something quite interesting. I never saw them again.

Joe Barnes (13)
Ysgol Bryn Alyn, Gwersyllt

The KFC Incident

Today, I fancied something different. So I went to the local KFC, ordered some food and waited patiently for my order to be called out. My order number was 373, so I had to wait a while. I ordered quite a big meal, 9 family buckets all for myself. While I was waiting, something strange happened in the kitchen; all their machines and ovens blew up and the whole place was on fire! The saddest part about it was I saw my order number showing up on the screen but we were told to evacuate the building. Very tragic!

Phoebe James (12)
Ysgol Bryn Alyn, Gwersyllt

I'd Won £1 Million

I finally found what I was looking for. It was right in front of me. Surely, he was there, he had to be. All of the clues had brought me there. I risked it all for this prize. Whoever found this man won £1 million. Nobody had made it this far. There was a brief creaking sound above me. I pulled away the debris to find a long, meandering flight of stairs. I slowly made my way up, one step at a time, not knowing what to expect. A shadow was visible from the room. I'd won the £1 million.

Kevy Parlour (15)
Ysgol Bryn Alyn, Gwersyllt

Room 355

I am a janitor at the famous Luston Hotel. Unfortunately, I have to clean up Room 355 in order to get a promotion. No one's entered that room since the deaths of the newly-wed couple. I heard they died from drowning or something. Tragic, right? Well, if you think that is tragic, I have to clean that room! No one has ever gone into that room since, so why should I? No one has ever come out. You can only hear their screams. I don't wanna die, I don't wanna go. Anyways, wish me luck now!

Victoria Bamgbala (13)
Ysgol Bryn Alyn, Gwersyllt

The Getaway

As the time started to limit, the risk increased. I had all the money from this successful heist. My friends had dropped dead. I quickly jumped in my car and loaded it up with the stolen bags of money, then sped off. The police slowly but surely caught up with me. I had to come up with something quick to get away. I saw a car dealership nearby and thought of a plan. I quickly hid my car and keyed a brand-new car. I had taken the number plate of it.
Nearly there. There was 1 mile to go...

Hermione Tudor (15)
Ysgol Bryn Alyn, Gwersyllt

The Underground Building

I woke up in a dark room underground with a plate on the door saying: 'Room 4, section 1'. When I sat up, I couldn't move my leg because it was covered in bandages. I stumbled out of the metal bed and looked for a light. I found an electric lantern and turned it on. All I saw was an empty room. I opened the door and tried to leave, but all I saw were 15-20 abandoned rooms and a sign showing the way. I found the exit and left to find an overgrown city. How long was I asleep?

Kacper Wachaczyk (13)
Ysgol Bryn Alyn, Gwersyllt

The Timer

As the clock hit 20 minutes, I knew the end was near. My competitors, more my friends, were struggling to live. I pushed forward but saw something we had overlooked. I saw a key in a book labelled with something we knew at the start. I saw the opportunity to take what I deserved. I could live a better life, but I looked up. Time was up. I saw the door slam shut and I saw my hopes go with it. I was trapped there to die and I deserved it. It was for all the times I wronged them...

Ben Diamond (13)
Ysgol Bryn Alyn, Gwersyllt

The Million Pound Heist

I had 20 minutes of fame on social media, then I was locked up in Cell 606. There were 4 of us, 3 of us were lying. Some of us were saying we'd won the million. We knew only one of us had. We were all being transported to the desert. We knew we had to tell the truth. We all owned up but they snitched on me, it was over.
16th July 2028, I have been locked away for 15 years. I have tried to escape 1266 times, but when I've tried to run, I have always been caught.

Tom Goodall (13)
Ysgol Bryn Alyn, Gwersyllt

The Mystery Death

It was Friday 22nd July 2012. It'd been a year since Anne's death. The police believed Anne was sick and chose to run onto the track, but why was her phone found on the highway? In the autopsy, there were signs of physical abuse, but Mr and Mrs Wilson weren't abusive. The summer was coming up and I had to do my report on something. So why not solve the mystery of why the once sweet, innocent girl would take her own life in such a tragic way?

Freya Hebblewhite (15)
Ysgol Bryn Alyn, Gwersyllt

Penny For Your Thoughts

I had recently won one million pounds. It was a life-changing event. Although, the one million pounds was paid in pennies and it was delivered by truck. The weight was too heavy for the truck, so the driver could not brake. So because they could not brake, it caused lots of structural damage. Cars, bikes and buildings were destroyed and I had to pay for it with the scattered pennies that were all over the crime scene.

Mason Robins (14)
Ysgol Bryn Alyn, Gwersyllt

YOUNG WRITERS INFORMATION

We hope you have enjoyed reading this book – and that you will continue to in the coming years.

If you're the parent or family member of an enthusiastic poet or story writer, do visit our website **www.youngwriters.co.uk/subscribe** and sign up to receive news, competitions, writing challenges and tips, activities and much, much more! There's lots to keep budding writers motivated!

If you would like to order further copies of this book, or any of our other titles, then please give us a call or order via your online account.

Young Writers
Remus House
Coltsfoot Drive
Peterborough
PE2 9BF
(01733) 890066
info@youngwriters.co.uk

Join in the conversation!
Tips, news, giveaways and much more!

YoungWritersUK **YoungWritersCW** **youngwriterscw**

Scan me to watch the Integer video!